This book was originally written back in my early twenties for my cousin Tyler Hargrove, prior to her birth. She is now graduating from high school this year... Yep, it sat on the shelf that long. The lesson we can all learn is to never give up and always follow your dreams!

-Vera Woodson

Lady Bug, Beetle Boy, and Friends: Bullies Be Gone!

Copyright © 2013 by Vera Woodson
Illustrations by Rafael Nazario

PRT1013A

Library of Congress Control Number: 2013945566

Printed in the United States.

ISBN-13: 9781620860496
ISBN-10: 162086049X

www.mascotbooks.com

Lady Bug Beetle Boy
and Friends
BULLIES BE GONE!

CREATED BY
VERA WOODSON

BEETLETOWN

Aunt Bee's
Honey Buns

Lady Bug
and Beetle
Boy live in
Beetletown,
USA. They live
in a beautiful
garden city where
they have friends
and family.

Lady Bug and Beetle Boy love to play on the playground after school.

"There is Bonnie Bee,"
says Lady Bug. Bonnie Bee
is Lady Bug's best friend.

Lady Bug and Bonnie Bee like to jump rope together.

Beetle Boy has a best friend, too. Speedy Spider is Beetle Boy's best friend. Speedy Spider has eight legs. One of his legs is broken. He hurt it while playing baseball.

"Here comes Sammy Snail!" shouts Beetle Boy.
"Let's play baseball!" says Sammy Snail.

Everyone goes to the playground
to play baseball. They make sure
to use safe equipment.

Speedy Spider can't play
because he has a broken leg.
"What's wrong, Speedy?"
asks Lady Bug.

"I can't play because I broke my leg,"
says Speedy Spider.

"That's okay," says Lady Bug.
"The fans are just as important
as the players," says Beetle Boy.

They all play baseball and
Speedy Spider cheers them on.

After playing baseball, they venture into the nearby forest to play hide-and-seek.

While Beetle Boy is counting,
all the others run and hide.
"...6...7...8...9...10! Here I come!"
yells Beetle Boy

Silence falls over the forest, then *SNAP!*
Beetle Boy hears a tree branch.

Uh oh, it's the Raggedy Roach brothers and now they have Beetle Boy cornered. They are going to bully Beetle Boy.

What should
Beetle Boy do?

Beetle Boy uses his voice to call out,

"Olly olly oxen free!"

As Beetle Boy calls out, all of his friends head toward him to find him cornered by the Raggedy Roach brothers.

What will they do?

As Lady Bug and friends are approaching, the sun shines between the trees. The Roach brothers see sunlight and they run and hide. They can't stand the sunlight, because it allows everyone to see their bad behavior.

"Let's get out of here!" yells Rudy Roach.
"I'm right behind you!" yells Roscoe Roach.

As the Raggedy Roach brothers run away, Lady Bug, Beetle Boy, and friends give each other high-fives for staying calm, coming together, and supporting their friend.

They all leave the forest and head to Aunt Bee's Honey Buns to tell her of the adventure. They know to always report bullying to an adult.

What Have We Learned?

A bully is a person who is mean to others.

True or False

A bully tries to make others feel bad.

True or False

A bully is someone who pushes and shoves other people.

True or False

A bully has a bad temper.

True or False

A bully needs help to control his/her behavior around other people.

True or False

NO BULLYING PLEDGE

I am not a bully. I am a good person. I make good choices. When I see someone being bullied, I must make sure they are safe by telling a teacher, parent, or adult.

Signed

_____

Vera Woodson is a child at heart. She is an educator with a passion for early childhood literacy. Working in schools keeps her young and watching students grow keeps her inspired. Growing up in Long Beach, California, the former Vera Pitts obtained her Bachelor of Arts degree from California State University, Long Beach. Mrs. Woodson obtained both of her graduate degrees in Education from the University of Virginia. "Woody", as she is known to her students, is married to her wonderful husband, Mark Woodson, and they currently reside in Falls Church, Virginia.